All children have a great ambition to read to themselves... and a sense of achievement when they can do so.

The **read it yourself** *series has been devised to satisfy their ambition. Even before children begin to learn to read formally, perhaps using a reading scheme, it is important that they have books and stories which will actively encourage the development of essential pre-reading skills. Books at Level 1 in this series have been devised with this in mind and will supplement pre-reading books available in any reading scheme.*

Children need to develop left to right eye movements and to perceive differences in word and letter shapes. Based on well-known nursery rhymes and games which children will have heard, these simple pre-readers introduce key words and phrases which children will meet in later reading. These are repeated and the full colour artwork provides picture clues for new words.

Many young children will remember the words rather than read them but this is a normal part of pre-reading. It is recommended that the parent or teacher should read the book aloud to the child first and then go through the story, with the child reading the text.

British Library Cataloguing in Publication Data
Murdock, Hy
    Old Macdonald's farm. — (Read it yourself. Fiction.
    Reading level 1; 1) — ([Ladybird books]. Series 777)
    1. Readers — 1950 –
    I. Title   II. Holmes, Stephen   III. Series   IV. Series
    428.6   PE1119
    ISBN 0-7214-0870-2

First edition

© LADYBIRD BOOKS LTD MCMLXXXV

Old Macdonald's Farm

devised by Hy Murdock
illustrated by Stephen Holmes

Ladybird Books Loughborough

A farm.

Old Macdonald
had a farm.

He had
some sheep.

He had
some cows.

He had
a tractor.

He had
some horses.

He had
some goats.

He had
some ducks.

He had
some hens.

Old Macdonald had a wife.

She had
some chicks.

She had
some lambs.

She had
a garden.

Old Macdonald had some children.

They had
some rabbits.

They had
some cats.

They had
some mice.

They had
a dog.

Here is
the house.

40

Here is
Old Macdonald
and his farm.

43